This Ladybird book belongs to

MarK Albert Toynton

PARK

Stories and rhymes in this book

Dotty learns to swim

It's fun to be five

Dotty and the spider

Let's pretend

Dotty's dancing lesson

Too busy

When I grow up

All Ladybird books are available at most bookshops,
supermarkets and newsagents, or can be ordered direct from:

Ladybird Postal Sales
PO Box 133 Paignton TQ3 2YP England
Telephone: (+44) 01803 554761
Fax: (+44) 01803 663394

A catalogue record for this book is available
from the British Library

Published by Ladybird Books Ltd
A subsidiary of the Penguin Group
A Pearson Company
© LADYBIRD BOOKS LTD MCMXCVIII

LADYBIRD and the device of a Ladybird are trademarks of
Ladybird Books Ltd Loughborough Leicestershire UK

Dinosaur Stories
for 5 year olds

by Karen King
illustrated by Jan Lewis

Dotty learns to swim

Dotty Dinosaur was bursting with excitement. Her fifth birthday was nearly here and all Dotty's friends were coming to her lagoon party.

Dotty couldn't wait to wear her special birthday swimming hat and splash about in the water. It was going to be brilliant.

There was just one thing bothering her…

"I wish I could swim without my armbands," she told her mum. "My lagoon party would be much more fun if I could really swim."

"Lots of your friends wear armbands, too," Mum said. "Don't worry, you'll have a lovely time."

"But I want to be able to swim," said Dotty. "I *really, really* wish I could swim."

"Well," said Dad. "There's no time like the present. Come on, you can have your first lesson now."

So Dotty and Dad trotted off to the lagoon.

Dotty swam really well with her armbands on, but as soon as Dad took them off she wasn't so sure.

"I'm s-s-scared. The water's too deep," she said, clinging to Dad.

"It's all right, Dotty, just swim to me and I'll catch you," said Dad, standing in front of her and holding out his arms.

But Dotty shivered with fright and clung to the side of the lagoon.

"I w-w-wish I could swim," she sighed.

Suddenly Dotty felt an enormous SPLASH beside her. It was her naughty brother, Joe. "Can't catch me!" he laughed, swimming off.

Dotty was cross and wanted to chase after him and splash him, too.

"I'll never do it," she said. "I'm just too scared."

"Never mind, Dotty," said Mum. "Put your armbands back on and we'll play ball." And Mum threw a big stripey ball into the water.

Everyone had fun playing ball.

Then Dad threw the ball and it landed on the other side of the lagoon.

"I'll get it!" said Joe, swimming off across the water.

"Bet I get it first!" shouted Dotty.

They both swam as fast as they could towards the ball…

Joe reached it first but before he could grab hold, it bobbed back towards Dotty.

"I've got it!" she shouted, clutching the ball.

Mum and Dad clapped. "Well done, Dotty," said Mum. "You swam across the lagoon – all by yourself."

Dotty looked puzzled. "But I've got my armbands on," she said.

Joe laughed. "They aren't blown up!" he told her. "Mum didn't close the hole and the air's gone out."

Dotty looked down at her armbands and saw that Joe was right. "You mean I *really* swam. All by myself?" she asked.

"You certainly did!" said Dad.

"Well done, Dotty," smiled Mum.

"Yippee!" shouted Dotty, and she pulled the armbands off and swam across the lagoon again, just to make sure!

"I *can* swim!" she laughed. "Now my birthday party is going to be the best party ever!"

And it was.

It's fun to be five

It's fun to be five,
There's lots to do;
I can ride my bicycle
And roller skate, too.

Being five is fun,
I can do so many things;
I can whizz down the slide
And go high on the swings.

Five is just great
For the things I want to do.
Five is just right
For a hug and cuddle, too!

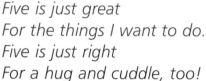

Dotty and
the spider

"Night, night, sleep tight," said Dad. He was looking after Dotty while Mum was out.

"Night, night," said Dotty.

But Dotty didn't feel ready for bed. She wanted to stay up a bit longer. She tossed and turned but couldn't sleep. So she crept downstairs.

"I can't sleep, Dad," she said.
"Can I have a drink?"

Dad gave her a drink and Dotty
padded back to bed.

She tossed and turned but she still
couldn't sleep. So she went
downstairs again.

"I can't sleep, Dad," she said.
"Can I have a biscuit?"

Dad gave her a biscuit and Dotty
padded back to bed. She tossed and
turned then looked up at the ceiling.
There was a big hairy spider
dangling just above her head! She
shrieked and ran downstairs.

"I can't sleep, Dad! There's a spider in my bedroom!" she cried.

"Hmm…" said Dad. "All right, come and show me."

But when they went upstairs the spider had gone.

They searched all over the bedroom, but couldn't find it.

"There was a spider, honest!" said Dotty. "I can't sleep at all now."

"Come on then," said Dad, smiling, and he let Dotty come downstairs for a little while.

When Mum came home, Dotty was still up. "Why aren't you in bed, Dotty?" she said.

"I can't sleep because there's a spider in my bedroom," Dotty told her.

"Really?" smiled Mum. "Something tells me you just wanted to stay up a bit longer."

Mum went upstairs to get ready for bed. Suddenly, she screamed… "AARGH!" and ran downstairs again.

"There's a big hairy spider in our bedroom!" she shrieked.

Dotty and Dad laughed.

"Come on," said Dad. "Let's catch that spider and put it outside. Then we can all go to sleep!"

Let's pretend

I'd like to be a princess
With a golden crown,
Looking so grand
In a silk cloak and gown.

I'd like to be a fisherman,
Out at sea,
Sailing in my boat,
Catching fish for tea.

I'd like to be an astronaut,
Going to the moon,
Waving from my space ship,
See you all soon!

There are lots of other things
That I would like to be,
But best of all
I like being **ME**!

Dotty's
dancing lesson

Today was a very special day.

Dotty was having her very first dancing lesson.

"Hello, Dotty," said Miss Prance, the dance teacher. "Welcome to the class."

Dotty watched as the other dinosaurs danced gracefully around the room. She couldn't wait to learn to dance.

"Right, everyone," said Miss Prance, "I want you all to dance on your tiptoes. Like this…"

Step, step, twirl. Step, step, twirl.

The other dinosaurs copied her.

Step, step, twirl. Step, step, twirl.

Dotty copied them.

Stamp, stamp, clomp! Stamp, stamp, clomp!

Everyone giggled. Dotty did feel silly.

"Never mind, Dotty, you'll soon get the hang of it," said Miss Prance.

"Now then, everyone," she said,
"I want you to dance on your tiptoes
then leap into the air. Like this…"

Step, step, leap!

The other dinosaurs copied her.

Step, step, leap! Step, step, leap!

Dotty danced after them.

Stamp, stamp, clomp! Stamp, stamp, clomp!

"Never mind, Dotty," said Miss Prance. "Keep trying."

Dotty didn't think she'd ever be able to dance as gracefully as Miss Prance and the other dinosaurs.
Her feet were just too clumsy.

"Right, everyone," said Miss Prance.
"Let's practise our steps again.
I want you all to dance two steps,
then twirl and leap. Like this…"

Step, step, twirl, leap!

The other dinosaurs copied her.

*Step, step, twirl, leap! Step, step,
twirl, leap!*

Dotty danced after them.

Stamp, stamp, clomp, thud! Stamp, stamp, clomp, thud!

Dotty burst into tears. "I'm just no good at dancing," she cried.

"That's not true, Dotty," said Miss Prance. "You need to find the right kind of dancing. Hold on, I've got an idea…

"I want you to tap your feet.
Like this…"

Heel, toe, heel, toe. Tap, tap, tap!

Dotty copied her.

Heel, toe, heel, toe. Tap, tap, tap!

"Hooray!" Everyone clapped.

"You see, you were doing the wrong kind of dancing," said Miss Prance. "You'll make a great *tap* dancer."

Dotty was delighted. She put on some tap shoes and danced happily across the floor.

Heel, toe, heel, toe. Tap, tap, tap!

Too busy

Today Dotty wanted to do something exciting.

"Can we go to the park?" she asked Mum.

"Not yet, I'm too busy," said Mum. "I've got these cupboards to paint."

So Dotty went to find Dad. Perhaps he'd take her to the park.

Dad was in the garden, mowing the lawn. Dotty had to shout really loud before he heard her.

"Can we go to the park?" she shouted.

Dad turned off the lawnmower. "Not yet, I'm too busy," he said. "I've got to mow the lawn."

So Dotty went to find her big brother, Joe. Perhaps he'd take her to the park.

Joe was by the shed, cleaning his new bike.

"Can we go to the park?" asked Dotty.

"Not yet, I'm too busy," said Joe, wiping the saddle. "I'm cleaning my bike."

Dotty sighed and went back into the house. Everyone was busy except her.

"I'll play on my roller skates until everyone's finished their jobs," she decided.

While she was looking in her toy cupboard for the roller skates, she found lots of toys she'd forgotten all about... her blue dinosaur fairy, Big Ted and Baby Alice. So she played with them instead.

A little while later, Mum, Dad and Joe came into Dotty's bedroom.

"We've all finished our jobs now so we can go to the park," said Mum.

Dotty looked up from her toys.
"Not yet, I'm too busy!" she said.

They all laughed.

"Well, let's go after lunch," said Dad.
"Then we'll *all* have time!"

When I grow up

When I grow up
I'll do just as I please,
I won't wash my ears
Or scrub my knees.

I'll stay up all night
'Til it's quiet and creepy,
So I don't go to bed
'Til I'm very sleepy.

I'll play ball in the house
Whenever I like,
And ride around
Ringing the bell on my bike.

When I grow up
I'll stay out in the dark,
And spend my time
Playing in the park.

I'll go on the slide
Again and again,
And swim in the lagoon
In the pouring rain.

When I grow up
I'll have lots of fun,
And i won't be bossed –
Not by anyone!